BIONICLE®
DESERT OF DANGER

BY GREG FARSHTEY

ILLUSTRATED BY
JEREMY BRAZEAL

SCHOLASTIC INC.

NEW YORK   TORONTO   LONDON   AUCKLAND   SYDNEY

MEXICO CITY   NEW DELHI   HONG KONG   BUENOS AIRES

ISBN-13: 978-0-545-11542-1
ISBN-10: 0-545-11542-6

12 11 10 9 8 7 6 5 4 3 2 1   9 10 11 12 13 14/0

Book designed by Cheung Tai and Henry Ng
Printed in the U.S.A.
First printing, April 2009

Mata Nui stood in a desert. He didn't know how he had gotten there. He wasn't even sure where he was. The only thing he knew was that he was a long way from home. Once, he had been the ruler of an entire universe. But everything he cared about had been taken from him by an evil villain. With his power gone, he couldn't save his people. Then the villain forced Mata Nui out of his universe and into this one. It seemed dangerous. He had already been attacked by some kind of beast. He had managed to beat it, but he wondered what other creatures might be hiding in the sands.

Mata Nui heard someone approaching. He turned and saw a small figure driving a vehicle. Mata Nui was amazed that the machine could even move. It looked like it had been made by nailing together pieces of other vehicles. Since he could not be sure who was a friend or an enemy on this world, he raised his sword.

"State your business," said the visitor.

"I am just a traveler," answered Mata Nui. "I'm looking for the nearest city."

The visitor laughed. "Then you better start digging. Here on Bara Magna, you're bound to find the ruins of one."

Mata Nui stared at him for a moment. Then the visitor laughed again.

"That was a joke," he said. "Well, to answer your question, the nearest village is Vulcanus. I've got some business there, if you want a ride. My name is Metus, by the way."

Mata Nui climbed into the vehicle. "Thank you for the offer. My name is . . . Toa Mata Nui."

Metus looked at his passenger. "Interesting name . . . ."

The two rode for a long time over the sand dunes. Now and then, Mata Nui would spot buildings in the distance. They were half-buried in sand. It looked like no one had lived in them for centuries.

Metus suddenly stopped the vehicle and pointed up ahead. Mata Nui could see movement in the sand. It looked like ocean waves, but there was no water anywhere around. "Uh-oh," said Metus.

"What is it?" asked Mata Nui.

"Its real name is very long," Metus answered. "By the time you finish saying it, you've already been eaten. So we just call them sand bats."

Metus turned the vehicle and they sped off over the dunes. Mata Nui looked back and saw that the moving sand was following them. It came closer and closer. Then the sand exploded upward.

"Look out!" yelled Metus. "It's attacking!"

Mata Nui hung on as Metus steered the transport into a sharp turn. He could see the sand bat now. It looked like a huge snake with bat wings and was at least 15 feet long. The creature had shot straight up into the air and now dove down toward the two travelers. It smashed into the transport. Mata Nui and Metus fell out, landing in the sand.

Mata Nui gripped his sword and prepared for a fight. He was sure the creature would attack them now that they were on the ground. Instead, the creature dove back into the sand and disappeared.

Metus was on his feet, trying to roll the transport back onto its blades before the sand bat came back. Mata Nui helped him, but he couldn't take his eyes off the spot where the monster had vanished.

"Where is it?" he wondered.

"Not here. That's what matters," said Metus, climbing back into the driver's seat. "Get in!"

"Too late!" said Mata Nui, pointing at the ground. It was moving again, and the waves were headed right for them. Mata Nui grabbed Metus, pulling him out just before the sand bat soared up again and crashed into the vehicle.

"Run!" shouted Metus.

Mata Nui thought that seemed like a good idea. He started running. A screech from behind him made him turn. The sand bat was flying right at him!

Just before the creature grabbed him, Mata Nui dove to the ground. The sand bat flew past and plowed into the dunes, vanishing below ground again.

Metus had turned back and helped Mata Nui get up. "There are caves over there," said Metus. "Maybe we can hide in them . . . if there isn't something worse already inside."

Mata Nui looked ahead. The caves were at least a mile away. They would never make it. "We're going to have to fight it," he said. "Keep your eyes on the ground. Maybe we can spot the creature before it attacks again. When it comes up, try and knock its mask off."

"Huh?" said Metus, confused. "Its mask? What mask?"

"Where I come from, beasts wore masks that made them do evil things," explained Mata Nui. "But if you knocked the mask off, the animal went back to being peaceful."

Metus started running toward the caves. He
scanned the sand for signs of the creature as he went.
"Around here the monsters don't wear masks . . . or
hats, or pants, or anything else. And they eat you
because they're hungry and you're nearby. Got it?"

Mata Nui frowned. Metus was right. He had to
remember that this wasn't home and things didn't
work the same way here. Forgetting that might get
him hurt, or worse.

The sand bat exploded out of the sand to their left. Metus ran toward the caves. Mata Nui stood, sword in hand, waiting for the creature to attack.

He didn't have to wait long. The sand bat screeched and dove at him. At the last second, Mata Nui dove aside and swung his sword. The blade hit the sand bat's wing, but did no damage. The creature disappeared under the sand again.

Mata Nui looked down at the sand, then at his sword. "Metus, this makes no sense!" he said.

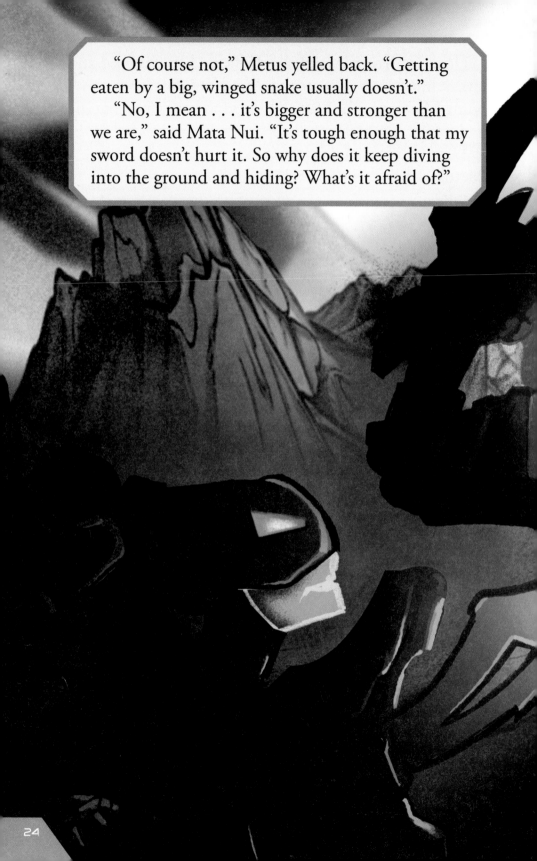

"Of course not," Metus yelled back. "Getting eaten by a big, winged snake usually doesn't."

"No, I mean . . . it's bigger and stronger than we are," said Mata Nui. "It's tough enough that my sword doesn't hurt it. So why does it keep diving into the ground and hiding? What's it afraid of?"

"Missing dinner?" said Metus. "How should I know?"
"Think!" answered Mata Nui. "What's around here?
Sand . . . rocks . . . air . . . ."

The sand bat shot up out of the ground right near Mata Nui, knocking him backward. As it dove at him, Mata Nui raised his sword to protect himself. The sunlight struck the blade. The creature suddenly turned away. Then it dove back beneath the sand.

"Sunlight!" Mata Nui shouted, jumping up. "It doesn't like the sunlight!"

"Boy, did it pick the wrong place to live," said Metus.

"This is what we're going to do," said Mata Nui. He told Metus his plan. The villager kept shaking his head as if Mata Nui were crazy.

The sand started to move again. This time, instead of running away, Metus and Mata Nui ran toward the spot where the sand bat would appear. The creature came up out of the ground. It flew into the sky, then dove at Metus.

As the sand bat headed for the ground, Mata Nui ran at it. He jumped and tackled the creature, knocking it off balance. The sand bat threw Mata Nui off easily.

Metus gave a yell and ran right in front of the sand bat. When it ignored him, he threw a handful of sand at it. The creature flew after him. Metus ran as fast as he could, but the sand bat was faster.

"Mata Nui!" Metus yelled. "Is this part of the plan? Because if it is, I don't like it!"

The sand bat suddenly turned back. Smoke was starting to come from its wings. It flew one way, but saw Mata Nui blocking its path. It flew the other, and Metus was there. Now its whole body was smoking.

The creature tried once more to get underground. This time, Mata Nui moved out of the way and let it go. It disappeared into the dunes in an instant.

"Wait a second!" said Metus. "You let it go!"

Mata Nui started walking toward the transport. "It didn't need to be hurt," Mata Nui said quietly. "It just needed to learn that the world it was visiting, the world above the ground, was dangerous. That's something I have to learn too."

Metus still wasn't sure who this strange visitor was or why he was here. But something told him he better stay close to this "Mata Nui."

Maybe I might learn something valuable, too, thought Metus. *Something very valuable indeed.*